Long e: ee

Queen Bee

by Liza Charlesworth

ISBN: 978-1-338-84440-5

Art Director: Tannaz Fassihi; Designer: Cynthia Ng; Illustrated by Michael Robertson

3 4 5 6 68 26 25 24

Printed in Jiaxing, China. First printing, June 2022.

SCHOLASTIC

Meet Dee!
Dee is a queen bee.

But Dee did
not like life as
a queen bee.

Bee, bee, bee!
Dee can see a lot of bees.
"I need to hide in my hive,"
said Dee.

“I need a nap,” said Dee.
Zzzzzzzzzzzzzzzzzzz!

Zzzzzzzzzzzzzzzz!
Dee is a deer!
But it did not feel nice.

Zzzzzzzzzzzzzzz!
Dee is an eel!
But it did not feel nice.

Zzzzzzzzzzzzzzz!
Dee is a jeep!
But it did not feel nice.

BEEP, BEEP, BEEP!
The jeep is on a street.

BEEP,
BEEP,
BEEP!
Dee woke up.

"I am NOT a deer, eel,
or jeep," said Dee.
"I am a queen bee!"
It DID feel nice.

Peek!
Bee, bee, bee!
Dee can see a lot of bees.

But Dee did not hide.
"I like life as a queen bee.
It is sweet!" said Dee.

Read & Review

Invite your learner to point to each *ee* word and read it aloud.

bee

need

deer

Dee

beep

meet

queen

sweet
peek
feel
eel
see
jeep
street
bees

Fun Fill-Ins

Read the sentences aloud, inviting your learner to complete them using the *ee* words in the box.

beep jeep Dee sweet bee

1. This story is about a queen ______.
2. The name of the bee is ______.
3. Dee dreams she is a deer, eel, and ______.
4. Dee's alarm clock said, "______, ______, ______!"
5. Dee said, "Life is ______!"